Author's note

Many years ago I lived with a Balinese family, in Bali. Kesuna and the Cave Demons is one of the stories they told me, and as far as I know, this is the very first time it has appeared in a book.

I have tried to picture the traditional life of the 'Island of Gods' here. On the first two pages you can see Bawang and Kesuna's mother and aunt pounding rice (the all-important food) to remove the husks. Grandad is petting his fighting-cock, and another aunt is making offerings for the guardian spirits from palm-leaf strips, rice and flowers. Grandma is putting some of these on the family shrine. She does not forget a little gift of rice for the underworld spirits, which the dog always eats. And in the background on other pages I have shown the temples, religious processions and festivals so important to the Balinese people. The invisible world of gods and spirits, witches and demons is truly part of everyday life too.

So maybe you can understand why Bawang and Kesuna are not at all surprised when animals talk to them and magical beings appear to reward or punish their actions. I hope you enjoy their story!

DUTTON CHILDREN'S BOOKS
Published by the Penguin Group
Penguin Books Ltd, 27 Wrights Lane, London W8 5TZ, England
Penguin Books USA Inc., 375 Hudson Street, New York, New York 10014, USA
Penguin Books Australia Ltd, Ringwood, Victoria, Australia
Penguin Books Canada Ltd, 10 Alcorn Avenue, Toronto, Ontario, Canada M4V 3B2
Penguin Books (NZ) Ltd, 182-190 Wairau Road, Auckland 10, New Zealand
Penguin Books Ltd, Registered Offices: Harmondsworth, Middlesex, England

First published 1995

1 3 5 7 9 10 8 6 4 2

Text and illustrations copyright © Gini Wade, 1995

The moral right of the author/illustrator has been asserted

All rights reserved. Without limiting the rights under copyright reserved above, no part of this publication may be reproduced, stored in or introduced into a retrieval system, or transmitted, in any form or by any means (electronic, mechanical, photocopying, recording or otherwise), without the prior written permission of both the copyright owner and the above publisher of this book

Filmset in Monotype Baskerville

A CIP catalogue record for this book is available from the British Library

ISBN 0-525-69040-9

Folk Tales of the World
A Balinese Folk Tale

Kesuna and the Cave Demons

RETOLD AND ILLUSTRATED BY
GINI WADE

DUTTON CHILDREN'S BOOKS

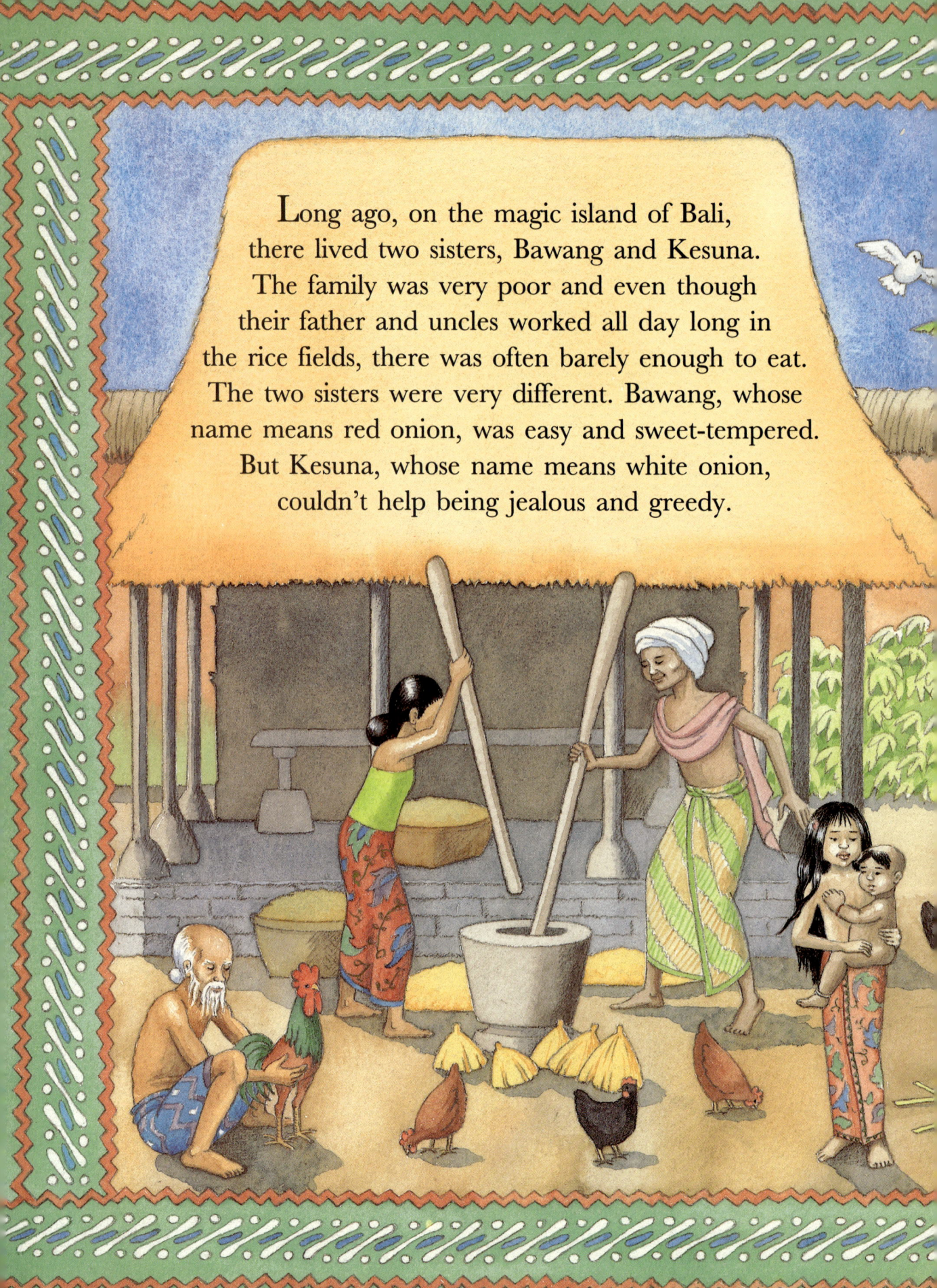

Long ago, on the magic island of Bali, there lived two sisters, Bawang and Kesuna. The family was very poor and even though their father and uncles worked all day long in the rice fields, there was often barely enough to eat. The two sisters were very different. Bawang, whose name means red onion, was easy and sweet-tempered. But Kesuna, whose name means white onion, couldn't help being jealous and greedy.

Every wash-day Bawang went down to the river with a basket of clothes. One day, as usual, she bathed herself in the fast-flowing water, then reached for a sarong to wash. But the basket had disappeared!

'Oh no!' gasped poor Bawang. 'Mother will be so cross if I have lost all our clothes.'

Bawang realized she must have placed the basket too near the water's edge and that it had tipped in, so she ran downstream as fast as her feet would carry her, to see if she could find it.

Bawang ran and ran, but still she could not see the basket. Tired out, she stopped to catch her breath. Two fish popped their heads out of the water to see who was puffing and panting so.

'Oh, fish, have you seen my basket of clothes in the river?' she asked.

'No sister, we have not seen your basket,' the fish replied.

Bawang ran on, tears running down her cheeks. She saw some frogs sitting on the river bank.

'Oh, frogs,' sobbed Bawang, 'have you seen my basket of clothes float by?'

'We regret, sister, that we have seen no basket of clothes,' croaked the frogs.

Bawang ran on further until she saw some crabs sunning themselves by the water.

'Oh, good crabs, please, you must have seen my basket of clothes passing by on the river?'

'No,' replied the crabs. 'We have not seen your clothes; but don't cry so, it's not such a loss. *We* don't need clothes.'

But Bawang could not stop crying. In fact, she sat on the bank and cried all the more. She saw a great golden bird sitting in a tree above her and she sang to him:

'Golden bird, golden bird,
I am so miserable I no longer wish to live,
Come peck me till I die.'

The bird was called Tjilalongan and he was not an ordinary bird. He flew down and pecked Bawang's head, but instead of blood, gold flowers appeared in her hair. Then he pecked her body and her sarong turned to gold. Bawang was amazed and overjoyed. She jumped up and cried, 'Now I can sell the gold and buy my family new clothes! Oh great bird, how can I ever thank you?'

'There is no need,' replied Tjilalongan. 'I have been watching over you, Bawang, and you are a good child. This is your reward.' And with this he flew off.

Bawang ran home and told her astonished family what had happened. Her sister, Kesuna, was jealous and decided she wanted some gold too. Why should Bawang have all the luck?

Next wash-day, Kesuna wrapped as many sarongs around her as she could and carried a basket piled high with her family's new clothes down to the river.

Kesuna let the basket float away on the river, and after a while she followed. She walked for many a mile, pretending to cry and hoping to see the golden bird, Tjilalongan. But he was nowhere to be seen. Soon she grew tired and was sobbing in earnest.

'My stupid sister must have been lying about the golden bird,' she cried. 'She must have stolen the golden flowers and sarong from somewhere, the wicked girl. Now I have lost all our new clothes and I can't go home until I have found them. It's all Bawang's fault!'

Tjilalongan, who had been following Kesuna, watched and listened, but kept silent.

Kesuna walked and walked until she saw a large cave. Curious, she tiptoed to the entrance. She peered in and saw two lights glowing in the dark. With a shock, she realized they were two eyes looking straight at her! She screamed and ran, but it was too late – an enormous hand shot out and grabbed her.

A huge demon and his hideous wife lived in the cave and they were delighted to have caught a human being. They locked Kesuna in a cage and pushed some boiled rice through the bars, but she felt too miserable to eat.

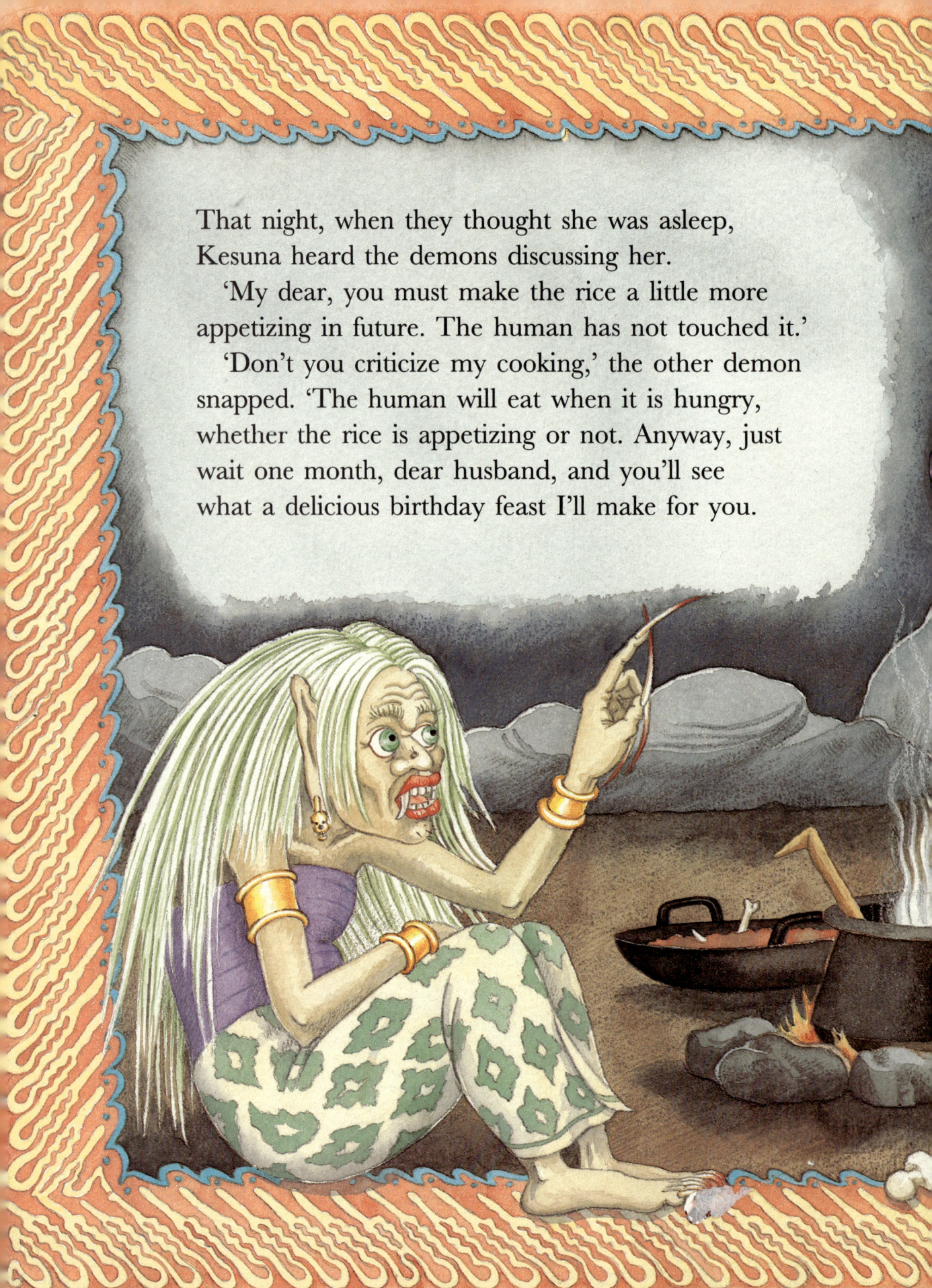

That night, when they thought she was asleep, Kesuna heard the demons discussing her.

'My dear, you must make the rice a little more appetizing in future. The human has not touched it.'

'Don't you criticize my cooking,' the other demon snapped. 'The human will eat when it is hungry, whether the rice is appetizing or not. Anyway, just wait one month, dear husband, and you'll see what a delicious birthday feast I'll make for you.

By then the human will be as fat as a sucking pig, and twice as tasty!'

With this happy thought in mind, the demons were soon fast asleep and thunderous snores shook the ground.

In her cage, Kesuna trembled and cried bitterly as she learnt of her horrible fate. Then through her tears she heard, 'Shh, don't cry, Kesuna!' Kesuna could not believe her ears. A tiny voice had spoken somewhere near her feet. She looked down. It was a little white ant.

'Tjilalongan, the magic bird, has sent me to rescue you,' the ant whispered. 'I will be back soon with help.'

Kesuna wondered how such a tiny creature could help her.

She watched in amazement as the ant came back with an army of friends who quickly nibbled through the bars. Kesuna wriggled happily out of the cage, gave the ants her heartfelt thanks, and ran out of the cave.

Kesuna raced along the riverbank until she reached home. 'Kesuna! We have been looking for you all night,' cried her father.

'We thought you had been drowned in the river, or eaten by a tiger!' sobbed her mother.

Kesuna told the story of her dreadful adventure. Everyone was so happy to see her alive and safe that not a cross word was said about the lost clothes.

Strange to say, this experience made such a deep impression on Kesuna that she changed completely. From that day on, she was never jealous or greedy again. Well, hardly ever!